ROADS

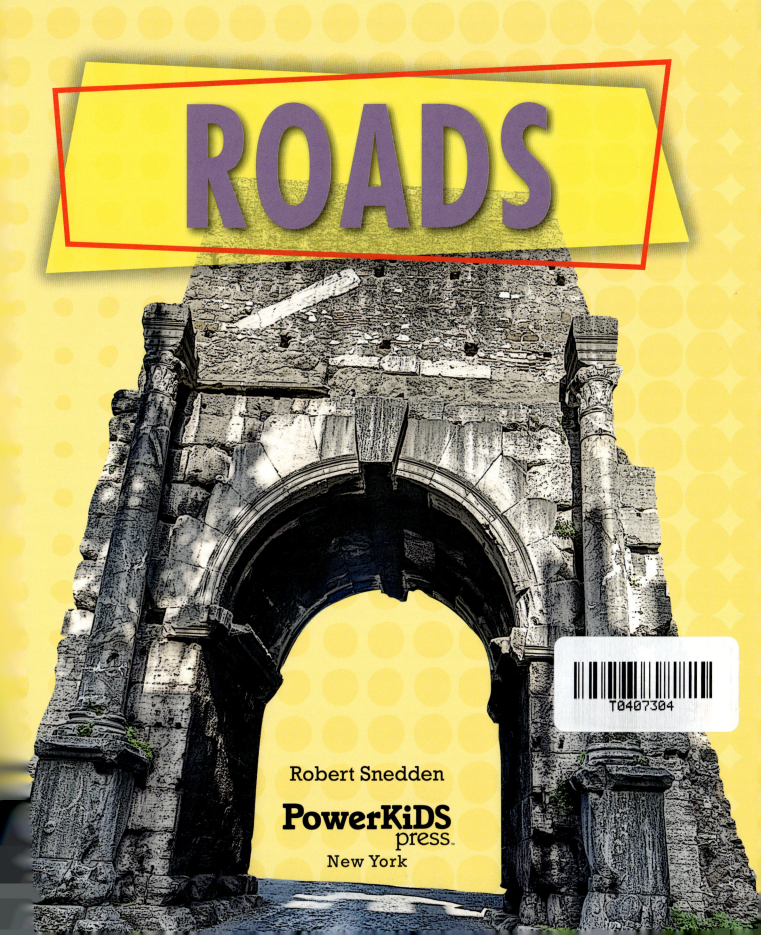

Robert Snedden

PowerKiDS press
New York

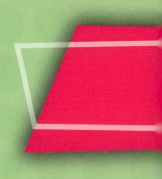

Published in 2017 by
The Rosen Publishing Group, Inc.
29 East 21st Street, New York, NY 10010

Cataloging-in-Publication Data
Names: Snedden, Robert.
Title: Roads / Robert Snedden.
Description: New York : PowerKids Press, 2017. | Series: Engineering eurekas | Includes index.
Identifiers: ISBN 9781499431018 (pbk.) | ISBN 9781499431032 (library bound) | ISBN 9781499431025 (6 pack)
Subjects: LCSH: Roads--Juvenile literature. | Roads--History--Juvenile literature.
Classification: LCC TE149.S64 2017 | DDC 388.1--dc23

Copyright © 2017 by The Rosen Publishing Group

Produced for Rosen by Calcium Creative Ltd
Editors for Calcium Creative Ltd: Sarah Eason and Harriet McGregor
Designers: Paul Myerscough and Jessica Moon
Picture researcher: Rachel Blount

Picture credits: Cover: Shutterstock: Elwynn. Inside: Venetia Dean 29 artwork; Pixabay: Antranias 28–29, Thomashendele 5b; Shutterstock: 06photo 20–21, Pola Damonte 15r, Everett Historical 18–19, Givaga 6b, Kamira 4–5, LovePHY 21r, Sinelev 11, Snvv 3, 22–23, Torook 10–11, Anibal Trejo 1, 12–13; Solar Roadways®: 26–27, 27b; Wikimedia Commons: Darafsh Kaviyani 9r, Ahmed1251985 17r, Colegota 14–15, Fabienkhan 8–9b, MatthiasKabel 12l, Ad Meskens 8–9t, MM 6–7, John O'Neill 5t, Royalbroil 23t, Stephencdickson 16–17.

All rights reserved. No part of this book may be reproduced in any form without permission in writing from the publisher, except by a reviewer.

Manufactured in the United States of America
CPSIA Compliance Information: Batch #BW17PK: For Further Information contact Rosen Publishing, New York, New York at 1-800-237-9932.

Contents

First Roads 4
Roads of the Ancient World 6
Long-Distance Travel 8
Ancient Amber Routes 10
Roman Roads 12
Inca Roads 14
The Path to the Modern Road 16
Age of the Automobile 18
Modern Road Building 20
Superhighways 22
Global Roads 24
The Future Is Electric 26
On the Road 28
Glossary 30
Further Reading 31
Index 32

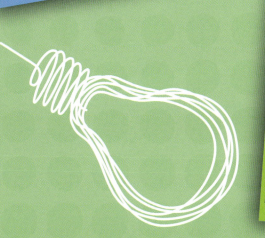

First Roads

The earliest humans had no need for roads. There were no permanent **settlements** and few regularly traveled routes. People simply followed where the animals went or searched for fruit and other plant foods. The first roads were paths. They were probably made by people following the tracks of animals they were hunting.

Settling Down

People began to build towns and villages when they started farming, about 12,000 years ago. This first happened in Mesopotamia, which was in the region of modern Iraq. **Agriculture** meant staying in the same place to look after crops and animals. People began to use roads, which made it much easier to move people and goods from one community to another.

Thousands of years ago, the **Assyrians** built roads to transport soldiers and weapons into battle.

The Wheel

The invention of the wheel brought a greater demand for paved roads. Wheeled carts and wagons became more common around 2000 BC. The availability of metal tools at the same time made cutting stone for road construction easier.

Early wheels were often heavy and crudely shaped.

ENGINEERING FIRSTS

The first roads began as well-traveled trails, like this one.

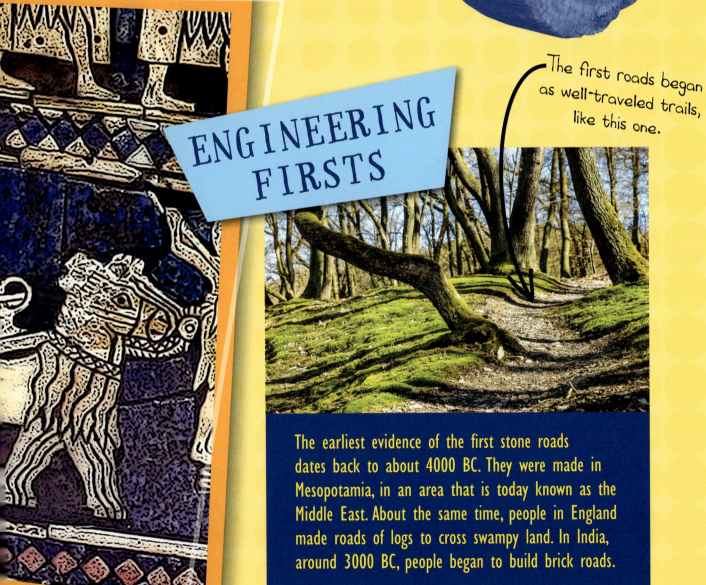

The earliest evidence of the first stone roads dates back to about 4000 BC. They were made in Mesopotamia, in an area that is today known as the Middle East. About the same time, people in England made roads of logs to cross swampy land. In India, around 3000 BC, people began to build brick roads.

Roads of the Ancient World

Most people in ancient Egypt lived close to a waterway. It was much easier to travel along the Nile River than to walk along a dry, dusty road. The wheel did not arrive in Egypt until about 1600 BC. Even after this time, wheeled vehicles for transportation were still rare. The ancient Greeks also built few roads. They depended mainly on sea travel and there is not much evidence that they built roads for travel and transportation.

ENGINEERING FIRSTS

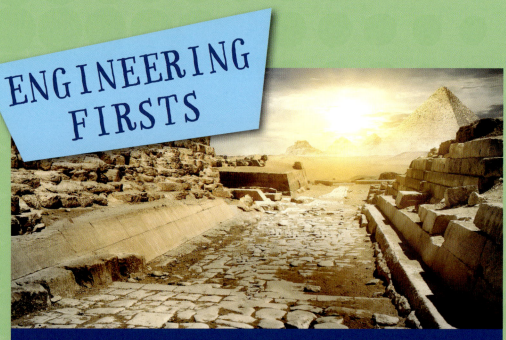

The first paved road dates back to about 2600 BC. In 1994, researchers investigating ancient Egyptian stone **quarries** found a road 6 feet (2 m) wide and 7 miles (12 km) long. It was paved with slabs of sandstone and limestone and a few logs of **petrified** wood.

The Egyptian paved road ran across the desert to the southwest of what is now Cairo.

Ancient Greek towns did have paved streets. This street ran through the city of Corinth.

Ancient Egyptian Paving

In ancient Egypt, the earliest paved road was built to make it easier to drag sleds loaded with **basalt**. The sleds were taken from quarries to waiting barges, which then took the stone to building sites. The sleds were probably pulled along on rollers.

Coast to Coast on Crete

Before the discovery of the Egyptian paved road, the oldest known paved road was on the Greek island of Crete. The builders of this road were the Minoans, one of the earliest civilizations in the Mediterranean. At the height of their power, around 1700 BC, they built towns with palaces and roads to link them. One road was 31 miles (50 km) long and stretched from coast to coast across the island. It was made of layers of stone set in plaster with a central line of basalt flagstones.

Long-Distance Travel

One of the first long-distance roads dates back to around 1200 BC. It connected the city of Susa, in present-day Iran, to the ports of Ephesus and Izmir. The ports were 1,200 miles (1,930 km) away in what is today Turkey. The road was more like a track than a proper road, but it was still very important for trade. In 670 BC, the Assyrian king decided that roads should be laid throughout the kingdom to make trading easier. Other rulers in the region soon did the same.

The Royal Road

The Persians became the major power in the region around 600 BC. The Persian Royal Road was built by the Persian King Darius I (c. 550–486 BC). It covered more than 1,500 miles (2,400 km). The road was of a poor quality. It was not paved and was made of **packed earth**, but large wagons still used it. Royal messengers were given priority on the road.

The Persian Royal Road stretched across present-day Iran, Iraq, and Syria and on to the coast of Turkey.

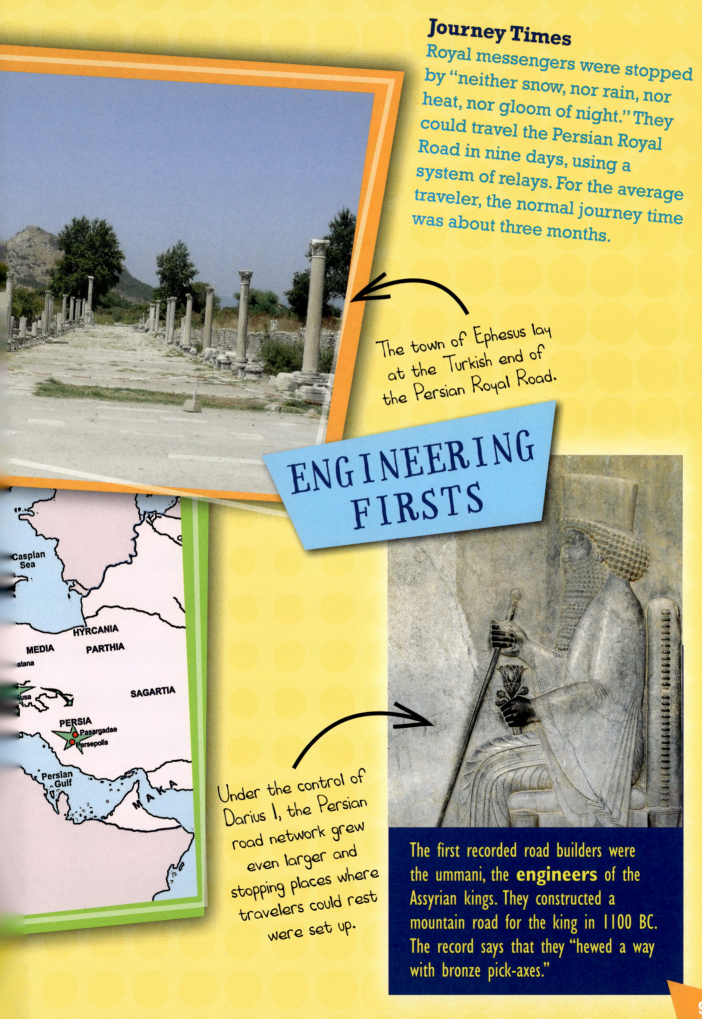

Journey Times

Royal messengers were stopped by "neither snow, nor rain, nor heat, nor gloom of night." They could travel the Persian Royal Road in nine days, using a system of relays. For the average traveler, the normal journey time was about three months.

The town of Ephesus lay at the Turkish end of the Persian Royal Road.

ENGINEERING FIRSTS

Under the control of Darius I, the Persian road network grew even larger and stopping places where travelers could rest were set up.

The first recorded road builders were the ummani, the **engineers** of the Assyrian kings. They constructed a mountain road for the king in 1100 BC. The record says that they "hewed a way with bronze pick-axes."

Ancient Amber Routes

Trade routes developed across Europe from about 2000 BC. By around 1500 BC, many of the routes crossing Europe had linked together to form what became known as the Amber Routes.

Trade

The Amber Routes were used by traders between 1900 BC and 300 BC. They were used to transport amber and tin from northern Europe to the Mediterranean. Amber is formed from fossilized tree resin, a sticky substance produced by evergreen trees. It was valued for its natural beauty and supposed magical properties. According to the Roman historian Tacitus (c. AD 56–117), the amber traders traveled everywhere in safety, even in wartime.

The oldest amber ever found dates back more than 300 million years.

Tracks

Like the roads of Assyria and Persia, the Amber Routes were not paved roads. They were little better than well-traveled tracks. Where the tracks crossed mountains, rivers, or swampy ground, logs were laid on them to make them easier to use. There is evidence that the oldest log roads were built before 1500 BC. A few remains of these roads have survived to the present day.

ENGINEERING FIRSTS

This forest path was made using centuries-old skills.

Log roads were constructed by laying down a bed of tree boughs and branches that could be up to 20 feet (6 m) wide. On top of these, logs were placed pointing in the direction of the road. This layer was then covered with a second layer of logs laid side by side at right angles to the previous layer. In the better-built log roads, every fifth or sixth log was fastened to the ground with wooden pegs. The logs were then covered with sand and gravel or turf, to give an even surface.

Roman Roads

The greatest road builders of the ancient world were undoubtedly the Romans (27 BC–AD 476). They brought together technical ideas from different cultures and, importantly, the Romans invented **concrete**. This was a major advance in road building. By the peak of the Roman Empire, they had built 52,800 miles (85,000 km) of roads.

ENGINEERING FIRSTS

The groma weights are steadied before use.

Roman road builders used a tool called a groma to help them be sure their roads were straight. The groma was made from two pieces of wood nailed together at right angles in a cross shape. Lead weights were hung from the ends of the crosspieces. By lining up one lead weight with the one at the opposite end of the crosspiece, they could be sure that they had a straight line.

Roman Road Building

To build a Roman road, first the builders dug parallel trenches about 40 feet (12 m) apart to provide **drainage**. Next, the **foundation** for the road was laid using material dug out from the drainage trenches and from land nearby. This foundation was then covered with sand or mortar (a mixture of volcanic ash, water, and lime) on which further layers were built.

Road Layers

Next, a layer called the statumen layer was added. This was 10–24 inches (25–60 cm) thick and was made up of stones at least 2 inches (5 cm) in size. The next layer, the rudus, was formed from an 8-inch (20 cm) layer of concrete made from smaller stones. Then a third layer was added that was made of concrete made from small gravel and coarse sand. This layer was about 12 inches (30 cm) thick. If the road was an important one, such as the Appian Way, large stone slabs were placed on top. The road sloped from the center to the outside edges to allow rainwater to drain off.

The Arch of Drusus stands near the beginning of the Appian Way, one of Rome's most important roads.

Inca Roads

From around AD 1100 to 1532, the Incas of South America built a road system that rivaled that of the Romans. It is one of the finest engineering achievements in the world.

Long and Wide

The Inca road system extended from Quito, Ecuador, through Cuzco, Peru, to Santiago, Chile. It included a 23-foot-wide (7 m) roadway more than 3,100 miles (5,000 km) long that followed the Andes mountain range. Although the Incas put a great deal of effort into road building, they did not have the wheel. All travel was by foot and pack animal.

Better than Europe

When the Spaniards arrived in South America early in the sixteenth century, they found 24,000 miles (39,000 km) of Inca roads. These covered an area of nearly 800,000 square miles (2 million sq km) and served a population of 10 million people. The Spaniards could see that the Inca roads were far better than the roads in Europe at the time.

Present-day travelers still use the old Inca roads.

ENGINEERING FIRSTS

This staircase climbs the side of a mountain near Machu Picchu, Peru.

The Andes route was an incredible feat of engineering. The road had galleries cut into solid rock with surrounding walls hundreds of feet high to support the roadway. It had suspension bridges that had wool or fiber cables to cross mountain streams and valleys. In steeper parts of the road, stone staircases were cut into the rock. Some mountain passes reached as high as 16,400 feet (5,000 m).

Following the Landscape

Unlike the long, straight Roman roads, Inca roads followed natural contours. Inca roads were built using wooden, stone, and bronze tools and whatever materials were close by. Flattened roadbeds were usually made using packed earth, sand, or grass. More important roads were finished with paving stones or **cobblestones**.

The Path to the Modern Road

After the end of the Roman Empire in AD 476, Europe's roads were not properly maintained for centuries. Transportation relied on pack trains. These were lines of horses or mules that could still move along the badly maintained roads where wheeled carts could not. From around the twelfth century, trade slowly grew between cities again. Then, good roads were needed to bring in food and other supplies.

Thomas Telford

The first real advances in road building since Roman times came in the eighteenth century. Thomas Telford (1757–1834) was born in Dumfriesshire, Scotland. He was a road builder and bridge designer. He built his roads with a stone surface that could withstand very heavy loads. His roads were 18 feet (5.5 m) wide and built in three layers. The lower layer, named the Telford base, was made from good-quality foundation stones that were carefully placed by hand.

Scotsman John McAdam (1756-1836), his three sons, and four grandsons were all road builders.

John Loudon McAdam

John Loudon McAdam began his road-building career in 1787. McAdam's road was raised above the surrounding surface to allow rainwater to run off it. The surface of the road was formed from small, sharp-edged stones that locked together as they were pressed into position. The stones used by McAdam were often referred to as "road metal." Roads made from the stones were called metaled or macadam roads. This method is still used in road building today.

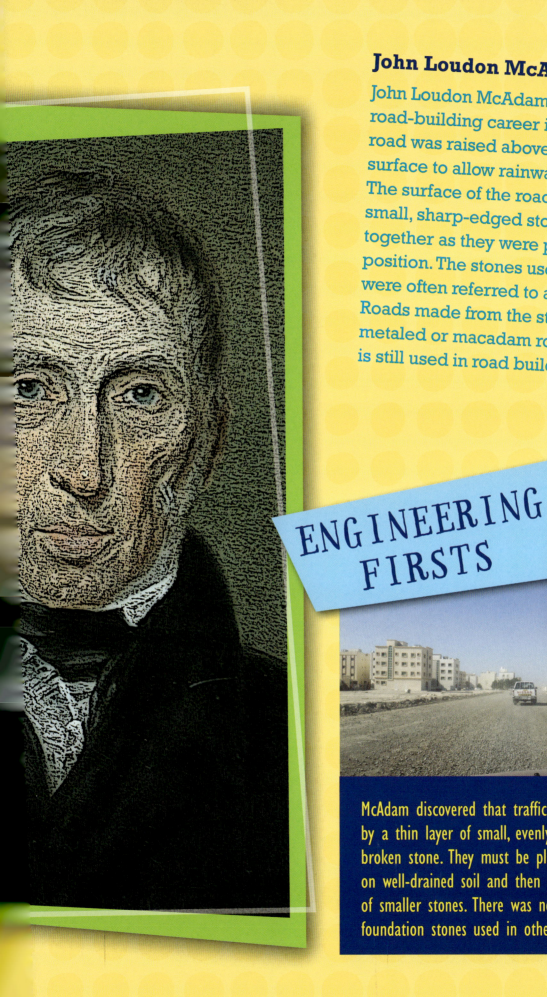

ENGINEERING FIRSTS

This present-day road in the United Arab Emirates was made using McAdam's techniques.

McAdam discovered that traffic could be supported by a thin layer of small, evenly sized pieces of broken stone. They must be placed and pressed down on well-drained soil and then covered by a surface of smaller stones. There was no need for the heavy foundation stones used in other methods.

Age of the Automobile

From the mid-nineteenth century until the start of the twentieth century, developing the railroads became more important than road improvements. The first road users to demand smoother surfaces were cyclists.

Bicycles and Automobiles

Cycling grew in popularity toward the end of the nineteenth century. Cycling organizations, such as the League of American Wheelmen (LAW), pushed for better roads. McAdam's roads were quite inexpensive, but they were difficult to maintain. They were also not suited to the needs of the automobiles and trucks that began to appear through the twentieth century. Stronger and tougher materials were needed. Materials that would help the tires of faster-moving vehicles grip the road were also important.

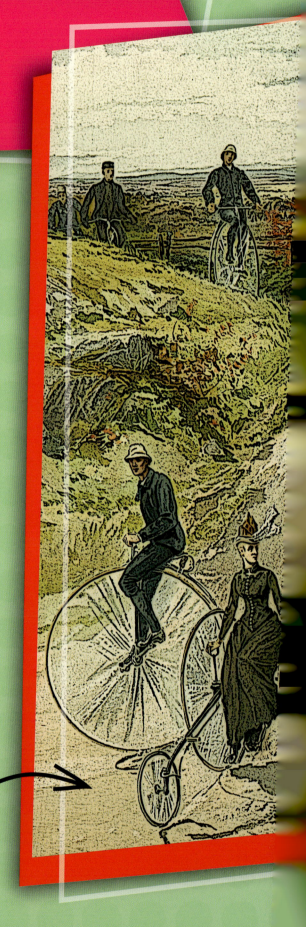

Riding penny farthing bicycles like these was very dangerous on an uneven road surface.

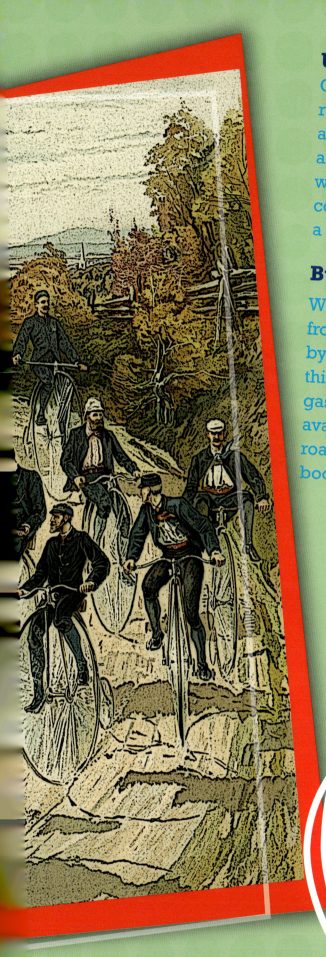

Using Asphalt

One material that proved just right for road surfaces was **asphalt**. Two forms of asphalt were developed: asphaltic concrete and hot-rolled asphalt. Asphaltic concrete was stiff and strong. Hot-rolled asphalt contained more **bitumen** and produced a far smoother surface.

By-Product

When kerosene (a fuel oil) is obtained from petroleum, bitumen is produced as a by-product. Gasoline is also a by-product of this process. The greater the demand for gasoline, the more bitumen became available to make asphalt for road building. This was a major boost for US road builders.

FUTURE EUREKAS!

Researchers are working on a self-repairing concrete. Capsules of a chemical called sodium silicate are put in the concrete mix. If a crack forms, the capsules break open and release a gel. The gel expands and hardens to fill the space, repairing the road.

Modern Road Building

A road engineer carefully studies the rocks and soil in an area before construction begins. Are the materials strong enough? Is the ground well drained? Will it shrink in dry weather? Unsuitable soils are dug out and removed, and then replacement materials are trucked in.

The Pavement

The **pavement** is the part of the road that carries the traffic. The top layer of the pavement is made of compacted (pressed) stone, asphalt, or concrete. It has to be smooth and provide grip for vehicles. Beneath this is a base of sand, gravel, and crushed stone that adds to the strength of the natural rocks and soils. In places where the natural soil is poor and the traffic is heavy, this layer may be more than 3.3 feet (1 m) thick.

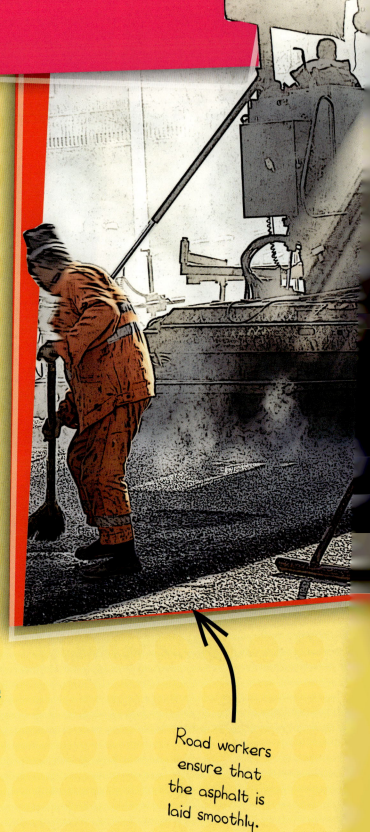

Road workers ensure that the asphalt is laid smoothly.

ENGINEERING FIRSTS

A cross section of a road reveals the different layers in its construction.

In 1901, British engineer Edgar Hooley (1860–1942) noticed a smooth stretch of road close to an ironworks. He discovered that a barrel of tar had burst open and waste slag from the nearby furnaces had been used to cover it up. Hooley **patented** the process of heating tar and adding slag and broken stones to form a smooth road surface, now known as tarmac.

Flexible or Rigid?

Pavements can be either flexible or rigid. Flexible pavements are built on broken stone, either pressed into place or combined with bitumen to form an asphalt. A paving machine, or paver, is used to add the hot bitumen in layers. The layers are then rolled smooth before the asphalt mix cools. Rigid pavements are made of concrete. Concrete shrinks as it hardens, causing cracks to appear. This is overcome by adding **steel reinforcements** to the pavement.

Superhighways

An expressway (also called a freeway or motorway), is a major road linking population centers. It has two or more lanes of traffic traveling in each direction. Opposing traffic lanes are separated from each other and there are controlled entries and exits from other roads.

Pennsylvania Turnpike

In 1940, the Pennsylvania Turnpike was completed. It was the first US freeway. The turnpike was designed for high-speed traffic and could accommodate the heaviest trucks. It originally ran from Harrisburg to Pittsburgh. It was later extended east to Philadelphia and west to the Ohio border, making it 327 miles (526 km) long in total.

The design of a complex interchange, such as this one in Shanghai, China, is almost a work of art.

FUTURE EUREKAS!

An intersection is where highways cross at the same level. In the future, driverless cars may make traffic flow much faster at intersections. Computer intersection managers will keep cars moving constantly without the need for red lights.

The Marquette Interchange in Milwaukee carries almost 300,000 vehicles per day.

Interchange Challenge

An interchange is where one road passes over another, with ramps to connect them. It connects freeways with other roads as well as with other freeways. The Marquette Interchange in Milwaukee links three interstate freeways. It was completed in 1968. Over time, it carried twice the traffic it was designed for. To solve the problem, the interchange was rebuilt. More lanes were added, ramps were redesigned, and **connector** roads were added. Bridges, walls, and fencing were improved. The project cost $810 million and was completed in August 2008.

Global Roads

Pan-American Highway, connects 20 countries in the Americas and includes the entire US Interstate System, 30,000 miles (48,000 km)

Trans-Canada Highway, Victoria, B.C., to St. John's, Newfoundland, 4,860 miles (7,820 km)

NORTH AMERICA

EUROPE

US Route 20, Boston, Massachusetts, to Newport, Oregon, 3,365 miles (5,415 km)

Interstate 80, San Francisco, California, to New Jersey, 2,900 miles (4,666 km)

US Route 6, Bishop, California, to Provincetown, Massachusetts, 3,205 miles (5,158 km)

Interstate 90, Boston, Massachusetts, to Seattle, Washington, the longest US interstate, 3,020 miles (4,860 km)

SOUTH AMERICA

What are the roads like where you live? Are they well maintained or in need of repair?

Do you think we need to build more roads? If we do, what problems do you think that might cause?

What do you think are the most important things to keep in mind when designing a new road?

Trans-Siberian Highway, St. Petersburg, Russia, to Vladivostok, Russia, 6,800 miles (11,000 km)

ASIA

China National Highway 010, 3,540 miles (5,700 km)

AFRICA

Golden Quadrilateral Highway Network, India, connects the four major Indian cities of Delhi, Mumbai, Chennai, and Kolkata, 3,408 miles (5,846 km)

Highway 1, Australia, the longest national highway, 9,000 miles (14,500 km)

AUSTRALIA

What effect might a highway have on the communities it passes through?

25

The Future Is Electric

What could the roads of the future look like? One idea is to replace asphalt with solar panels. The panels would produce energy, light up the road, and melt snow. They could even recharge electric-powered cars as they drive along.

Solar Roadways

The idea for solar roadways comes from Julie and Scott Brusaw of Idaho. They propose building a high-strength road surface with solar collector cells, **LEDs**, and heating elements embedded within it. The LEDs will give directions and light the road at night. The heating elements will keep the road from icing up in winter. Beneath this, an electronic layer will turn solar energy into electricity. There will be **sensors** that monitor the temperature of the upper layer and activate the heating elements when needed. Microprocessors will control the lighting on the road surface. This layer will be the "brain" of the solar highway.

Solar road LEDs could make journeys easier by marking out a detour to avoid a stationary object or an accident.

Plastic Roads?

With huge numbers of vehicles driving over them, asphalt roads deteriorate over time and need expensive maintenance. A Dutch company has suggested that one solution would be to develop and construct plastic roads. The idea is that they would be installed in sections that are as easy to remove and replace as they are to install. The road sections would also have space inside for water and gas pipes and electric cables.

FUTURE EUREKAS!

In 2016, France announced plans to cover 620 miles (1,000 km) of roads with solar panels. The panels should be strong enough to support fully loaded trucks. A 0.6-mile (1 km) stretch of panels can generate enough power to supply a town of 5,000 people.

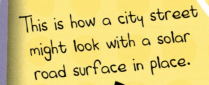

This is how a city street might look with a solar road surface in place.

On the Road

We will always need a way of getting people and goods from one place to another. Over thousands of years, roads have proven to be a very good way of doing just that. The problem today is that there are so many people who want to use roads that sometimes the roads just cannot handle the traffic. The result is traffic congestion and roads badly in need of repair. What is the solution?

The Road Goes On?

Can people really go on building new roads? There are already an estimated 21 million miles (33.5 million km) of roads on our planet. That is enough to go around Earth 833 times! It is now necessary to find ways to make roads that are harder wearing, more environmentally friendly, and as efficient at getting traffic moving as possible. It is not an easy task, but people are always going to want to go places.

This cross section through a Roman road may give you some ideas for constructing your own Roman road (see page 29).

Be an Engineer

You can find out for yourself how the different layers made up a Roman road with this simple activity.

You Will Need:
- A shoebox lid
- Sand
- Small stones or gravel
- Larger stones
- Plaster of Paris
- All-purpose white glue

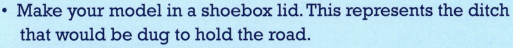

- Make your model in a shoebox lid. This represents the ditch that would be dug to hold the road.
- Brush a thin layer of glue over the inside of the lid and sprinkle sand over it. This is your first road layer.
- When the sand layer is dry, brush some glue over three-quarters of it and sprinkle on the gravel. This is the second layer.
- Next, the Romans added concrete. Instead, you could use plaster of Paris or a mix of glue and sand. Spread your "concrete" over half the shoebox road surface.
- Finally, add flat stones and glue them over half of the "concrete" layer. Now you have a Roman road model with every layer visible.

Glossary

agriculture The practice of farming, including growing crops and rearing animals.

asphalt A mixture of bitumen with sand or gravel used for surfacing roads.

Assyrians The people of ancient Assyria, a kingdom in the Middle East from around 2000 to 600 BC.

basalt A type of dark, fine-grained volcanic rock.

bitumen A thick, black liquid, either found naturally or obtained from petroleum.

cobblestones Small round stones used to cover a road surface.

concrete A mixture of sand, stones, cement, and water.

connector A road that connects one road to another road.

drainage A system for the removal of unwanted water.

engineers People who use science to design structures.

foundation The part of a road below ground level that supports its weight.

groma A Roman surveying instrument used to make straight lines and right angles.

LEDs Light emitting diodes; electronic devices that produce light when an electric current passes through them.

packed earth Earth that has been pressed together into a hard, solid mass.

patented Claimed the legal rights to an idea.

pavement The hard surface of a road or street.

petrified A once living thing that has changed into a stony substance over millions of years.

quarries Deep pits from which stone or other materials are extracted.

reinforcements Things added to make a construction stronger.

sensors Devices that detect and measure something, then record or react to it.

settlements Places where people live, such as villages, towns, or cities.

steel A strong metal made from iron and carbon.

Further Reading

Books

Brooks Bethea, Nikole. *High-Tech Highways and Super Skyways*. North Mankato, MN: Capstone Press, 2016.

James, Simon. *Ancient Rome* (DK Eyewitness). New York, NY: DK Children, 2015.

Proudfit, Benjamin. *The Pan-American Highway*. New York, NY: Gareth Stevens, 2016.

Stefoff, Rebecca. *Building Roads*. New York, NY: Cavendish Square, 2015.

Websites

Due to the changing nature of Internet links, PowerKids Press has developed an online list of websites related to the subject of this book. This site is updated regularly. Please use this link to access the list:
www.powerkidslinks.com/ee/roads

Index

A
Amber Routes, 10–11
ancient Egypt, 6–7
ancient Greeks, 6
Appian Way, 13
asphalt, 19–21, 26–27
Assyrians, 8–9

B
bitumen, 19, 21
Brusaw, Julie and Scott, 26

C
China National Highway 010, 25
concrete, 12–13, 19–21, 29
cyclists, 18

D
drainage, 13, 17
driverless cars, 22

E
expressway, 22

F
foundation, 13, 16–17
freeway, 22–23

G
Golden Quadrilateral Highway Network, 25
groma, 12

H
Highway 1, 25
Hooley, Edgar, 21

I
Incas, 14–15
interchange, 23
intersections, 22–23
Interstate 80, 24
Interstate 90, 24

L
logs, 5–6, 11

M
macadam roads, 17
Marquette Interchange, 23
McAdam, John Loudon, 17–18
Minoans, 7
mortar, 13

P
Pan-American Highway, 24
pavement, 20–21
Pennsylvania Turnpike, 22
Persian Royal Road, 8–9
Persians, 8–9
plastic roads, 27

R
road metal, 17
Roman, 10, 12–16, 29

S
self-repairing road, 19
solar panels, 26–27

T
Tacitus, 10
tarmac, 21
Telford, Thomas, 16
Trans-Canada Highway, 24
Trans-Siberian Highway, 25

U
ummani, 9
US Route 6, 24
US Route 20, 24